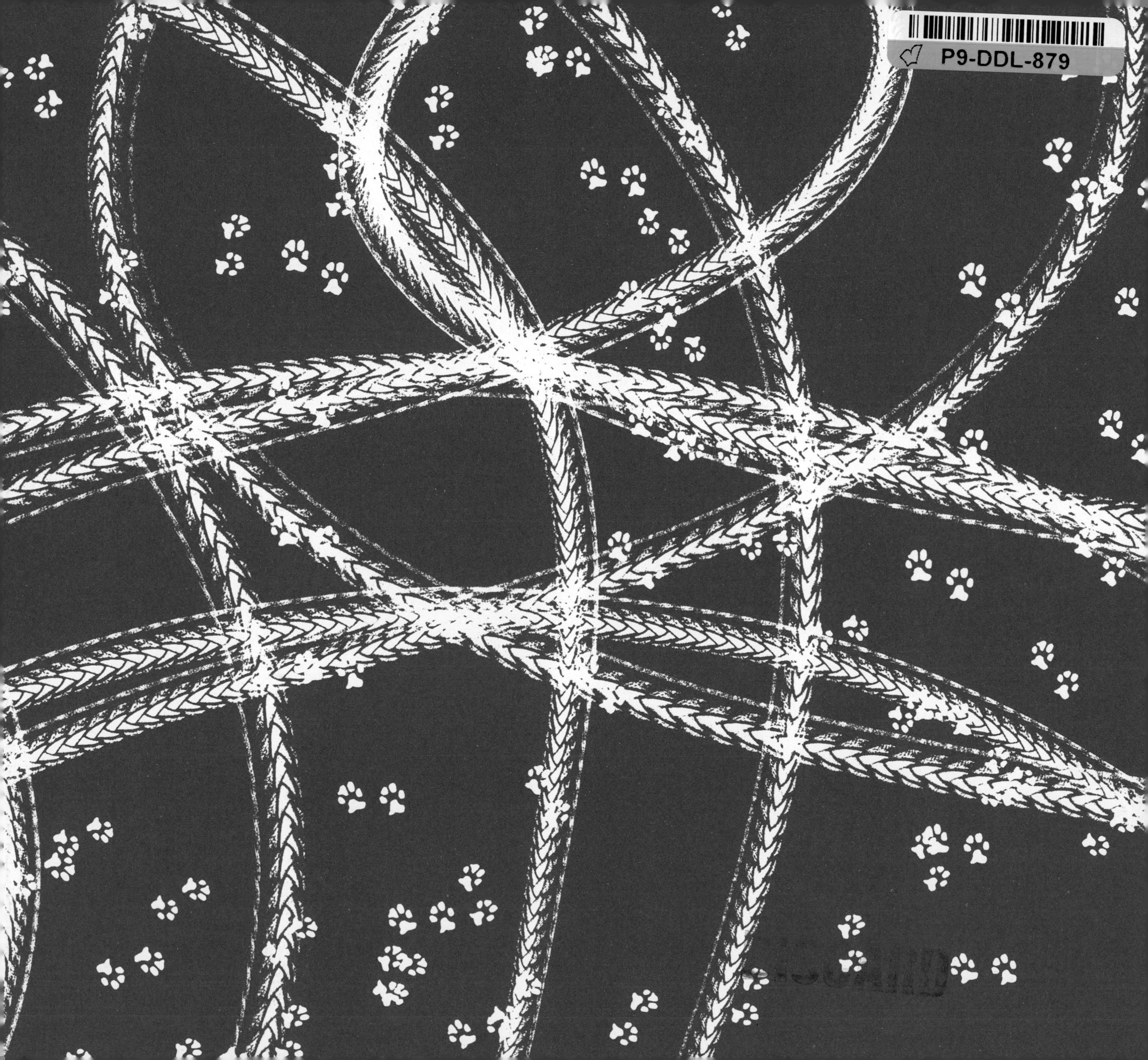

BEST DAY EVER!

by Marilyn Singer • Illustrated by Leah Nixon

Clarion Books

Houghton Mifflin Harcourt
Boston New York

Wake up happy, have a stretch.
Then I sniff the air.

Lick your face a bunch of times,
glad that we're a pair.

Best day ever!

After breakfast, time to dig.
Got a special box.

Find a bone, a tennis ball,
and some dirty socks.

Best day ever!

There's a kitty in the yard.
Chase it up a tree.

Let that cat know I'm the boss—

till she chases me.

Best day ever!

Steal a Frisbee from a pooch
where we go to run.

Eat a hot dog off a bench
(but I leave the bun).

Best day ever!

Head up farther in the park,
swim across the lake.

Scare away some wiggly thing.
Heard it's called a snake.
Best day ever!

Race through puddles full of mud,

love the way they squish!

Roll on something that smells great—
it's a nice dead fish.
Best day ever!

Quickly jump on my best friend.
He begins to yell,
"Down, girl! You get off me!
Phewy, what's that smell?"

Not the best day ever.

Hate this tub, this kind of wet,
and the taste of soap.

Will this bath be over soon?
Something tells me nope.
Not the best day ever.

Done at last, I give a shake
'cause I'm feeling damp.

Bump a table and, oh no,
I knock down a lamp!
Not the best
day ever.

Then my best friend hollers,
"Now what did you do?"

Tuck my tail and slink away,
feeling really blue.

Worst
day
ever.

Later on he finds me,
curled up on a rug,

snuggles close, pets my head,
offers me a hug.

Not the worst day ever.

"I'm sorry that I shouted.
I know it wasn't cool.
I think we need more lessons.
We'll go to training school."
Not the worst day ever.

JULY 6

"Nothing's broken, you smell nice,
everything's okay."

"Hurry," he says. "Bring your ball.
Let's go out and play."

Best

day ever!

© Steve Aronson

Author's Note

Whenever I'm asked what my favorite animal is, I answer, "A dog!" I've had many dogs. It was my late great standard poodle, Oggi, who inspired this book. We were in the woods and he was running around, sniffing everything and grinning. I could just hear him saying, "This is the best day ever!" But when you're a dog, things change quickly. My latest dog, Bizzy, can tell you this is true. Recently, she had a nice stroll in our neighborhood, which took her to the groomer—where she had to have a dreaded bath and a haircut—then home again with me to biscuits and her comfy couch. Her day went from best to not-so-hot to delightful in just a few hours! She definitely lives in the moment—which is something I wish I could do too!

© Grace Nixon Peterson

Illustrator's Note

When I read the words to this book, I nearly fell out of my (wheel)chair. It feels like the best book for me to illustrate! My life tends to revolve around three things: dogs, drawing, and life in a wheelchair. I have a little terrier-Chihuahua mix named Lucy who is exactly like the dog in this book. I love going to the dog park with her, where I can push my wheelchair while she runs alongside me off leash. I ended up in a wheelchair when I was 29, from a construction accident. I can't feel or move my legs or abdomen anymore, but a wheelchair provides a way for me to move around, and I have other adaptations that make me quite independent. Although I can do most things on my own, there is hardly a moment when I'm not dealing with my injury in some way. I've even trained Lucy to help me pick things up. I have had a "ball" working on this book—especially getting to use myself and Lucy as models, and visiting dog parks in my city for inspiration!

To the late, great Oggi and to the latest, greatest Bizzy.
—M.S.

For my Mom, who always knew I'd illustrate a book someday.
To Dad, who passed along a skilled hand and an amazing amount of grit.
And to all who helped me beat death and learn to thrive with a spinal cord injury—including my furry friends.
—L.N.

Clarion Books, 3 Park Avenue, New York, New York 10016

Clarion Books is an imprint of Houghton Mifflin Harcourt Publishing Company.

hmhbooks.com

The illustrations in this book were done in Procreate on an iPad. The body text was set in Lunchbox. Interior design by Celeste Knudsen

Library of Congress Cataloging-in-Publication Data is available.
ISBN 978-1-328-98783-9

Manufactured in China
SCP 10 9 8 7 6 5 4 3 2 1
4500818563

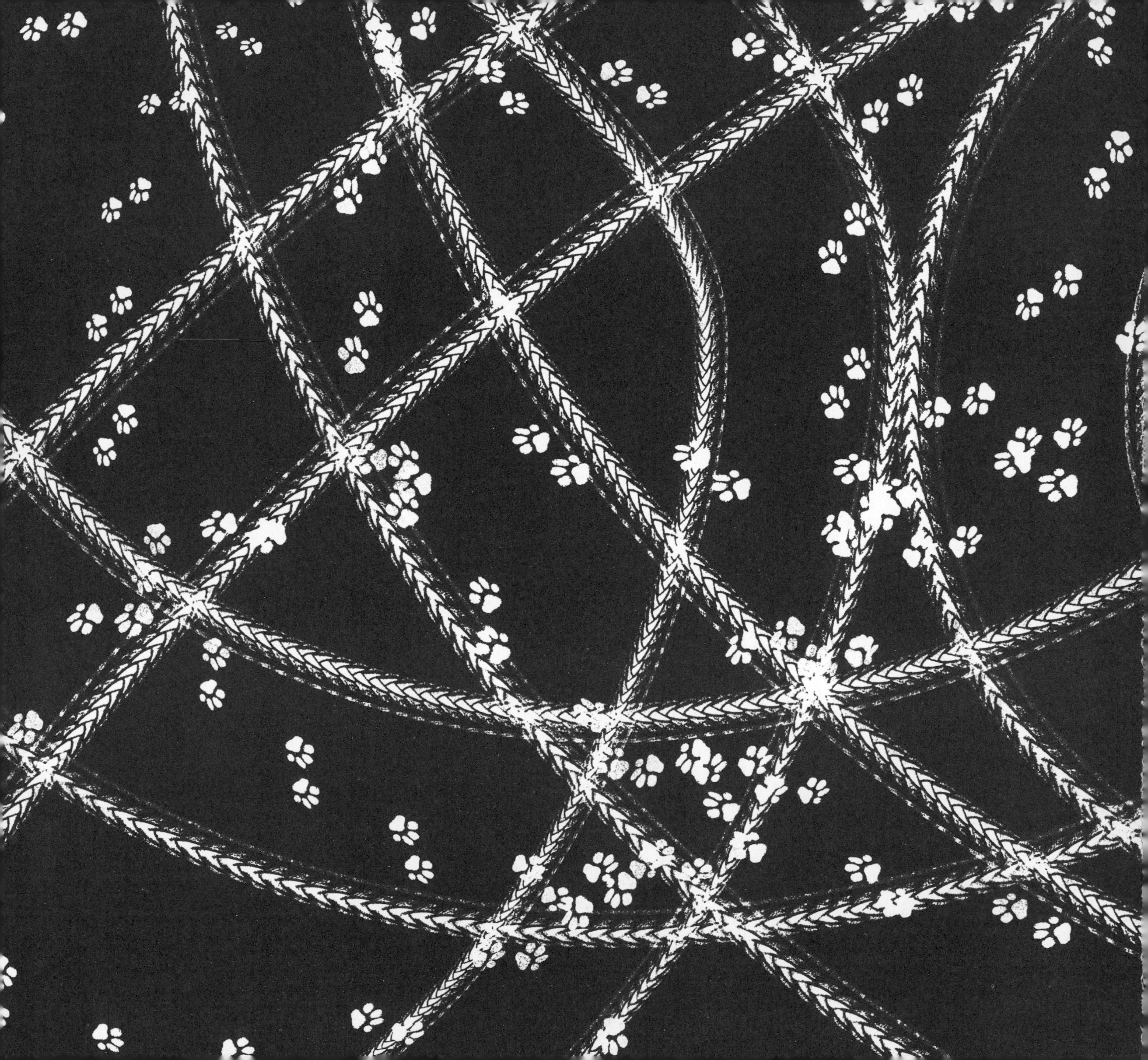